Praise for *Who's Your Daddy*

How does a lyric memoir—a queered-up autobiographical hybrid of prose and poetry—become a real page-turner? Well, for one thing, its speaker uses her authenticity and open-heartedness to generate a rib-cracking amount of courage to look for, find, and emotionally confront a missing Guyanese father who ends up being the "unhello" of a "nevermind." What's so moving about this discovery is the speaker's lyric response. It's a shrug that's a song that's the speaker telling it experimentally-straight about how it feels to have "arms free of fathers." It's a story that's a song that's the speaker's "gangster swagger" that beautifully tells of how to confront one's relation to "a culture of deadbeats, wannabes, has-beens, what-ifs, [and] can't-shows" without succumbing to despair. One really wants to quote Plath's line here about "eat[ing] men like air." Oh, I love the courage of this book. The whole "black heart" and love-strength of it. And you will too!
           **—Adrian Blevins, *Appalachians Run Amok***

A lyric anthem for the fatherless, for seekers of the places and people that made us, for the artists ready to unearth and reshape their own stories. I gulped this exquisite manual like precious medicine, a spell that made me more myself.
           **—Melissa Febos, *Abandon Me***

Collaborative, interactive, this work of poetry and memoir offers life as a recurring question. *Who's Your Daddy* is a study of how power and loss work on the intimate scales of daily living and queer loving. Read this with compassion for your own defining questions and the raw texture they have left upon your heart.
           **—Alexis Pauline Gumbs, *Dub: Finding Ceremony***

*Who's Your Daddy* is striking and gorgeous. "I'm born into a bracket of boys," White writes, framing a portrait of fatherhood that shutters and aches; it enthralls. I wanted to lap it up. A reflection on family that permeates via knitted prose with deep verse—my favorite kind. White's work is sonic, lyric, and important. I can't wait for y'all to read this book. **—Emerson Whitney,** *Heaven*

Who's Your Daddy

## Also by Arisa White

*You're the Most Beautiful Thing that Happened*
*A Penny Saved*
*Hurrah's Nest*
*Black Pearl*

## With Laura Atkins, Illustrated by Laura Freeman

*Biddy Mason Speaks Up*

# WHO'S YOUR DADDY Arisa White

Augury Books • New York

*Who's Your Daddy* © 2021 Arisa White
ISBN-13: 978-1-936767-61-8

Cover image: "The Drinking Gourd" (2018), courtesy of Sydney Cain, graphite on paper, 9″ × 12″. Author photo by Nye' Lyn Tho. Design by Shanna Compton. Edited by Kate Angus. Published by Joe Pan.

Augury Books is committed to publishing works of high literary merit, and in that spirit, offer this book of memoir/creative nonfiction to our readers. However, the experiences set forth here, and the words used to describe them, are the author's alone. Names and events have been altered and time frames merged to better represent the emotional and spiritual contours of the author's memories, as she sees fit to represent them.

Published in the United States of America by:
Augury Books
154 N 9th St #1
Brooklyn, NY 11249
www.AuguryBooks.com
info@AuguryBooks.com

Distributed to the trade by Small Press Distribution / SPD: spdbooks.org

Library of Congress Cataloging-in-Publication Data

Names: White, Arisa, author.
Title: Who's your daddy? / Arisa White.
Other titles: Who is your daddy?
Description: First edition. | Brooklyn, NY : Augury Books, [2021] |
    Summary: "A lyrical, genre-bending, coming-of-age tale featuring a
    young, queer, black, Guyanese American woman who, while seeking to
    define her own place in the world, negotiates a difficult relationship
    with her father"-- Provided by publisher.
Identifiers: LCCN 2020018568 | ISBN 9781936767618 (paperback)
Subjects: LCGFT: Poetry.
Classification: LCC PS3623.H5696 W48 2021 | DDC 811/.6--dc23
LC record available at https://lccn.loc.gov/2020018568

First Edition

## Prologue

**This is a grandfather feeling:** Hear these walls convert into a perpetual bloom of cherry blossoms. Petals as understudies for tears in constant descent when repressed grief climbs up my mother's chest. The grief is her father's shape. She never heard his "I love you." Cheated with a white woman, gambled away and didn't pay taxes on the family house, his bags brimmed with hurt shirts and broken trousers.

My mother's petals: "Dad, remember you used to take me to the bar."

My mother's petals: "In return, all the men I lust, I let break me."

My mother's petals: "It's difficult to say 'I love you.'"


I move
at the durational speed
of this grief-water,
a rhythm that suits
The Running Man.

# I.

"Blood follows the veins."
—Guyanese proverb

**My mother is nineteen** when she meets Gerald. Handsome, tall, good healthy teeth, dressed sharp and debonair, he could steal the room. She felt lucky he chose her. Ten years her senior and she smiles, mostly to herself, remembering him teaching her how to drive. All the places she goes. In his Cadillac down Fulton Street, down Nostrand Ave, without question up and down Atlantic and Pacific, DeKalb, on Eastern Parkway, through Gates and Myrtle, Bushwick and Halsey, sunsets on Jay. Down this first day of spring, red lights every two minutes when contractions start. The cab ride stretches out before the hospital. I am her second child. She has calm nerves, clear expectations, controlled breath. An easy birth. And what she negotiated with Gerald, a married man, about his role in my care—definitely included a one-way street.

**I feel for the father,** for a feeling of father,
I send out a cry, I am up when I hear my uncle
come through the door of the family house,
with the cherry tree out front, past midnight,
he walks up the stairs, then down the stairs,
and I'm the rock-a-bye baby in his arms.

At a time opened to the mythical world,
he dishes out Chinese takeout. I suck the knuckle of an
almost-eaten chicken bone. The fried rice glistens
from two packets of duck sauce. My uncle makes sure
each grain leaves me fed. When wee hours nod me out,
I am in his Tree of Heaven arms and the cradle never falls
into whole dead sounds or, thankfully, nothing at all.

**I'm born into a bracket of boys.** Five years before and five years after. There I stand in the middle of my cousins and oldest brother, all with the same middle name—Corey—as sisters are wont to do when they know they are having boys at similar times. Unite them in names as my brother and I bear maternal White. We're posing on somebody's stoop. It's summer and it looks so very eighties, the boys in runner's shorts with white piping, tube socks pulled up to kneecaps, three colored stripes at the top. Seven variations of short afros, and each one of them rocking Adidas or Chuck Taylors. Ice cream truck singing its jingle in the background of this photo, laughter and shit talking no doubt. A block party with classic R&B tunes like "We Are Family." The boys, staring off in different directions, and I'm cheesing at the camera.

**A SWAT team raids our Florida apartment** and the fact that I remember startles my mother to this day. I am three. We just moved in and there is no furniture. All bare and white walls. Officers kick in doors, slam open, knock down, tear shit off. An automatic gun points at me. My eyes on that black metal Cheerio. We're commanded not to move, but what move can we not make? Even this stillness we *moved* ourselves to do. I hold my bowels until officers evacuate our home with all our men in handcuffs. My stepfather Bing is the last one out. I leave my mother and baby brother sitting on the living room floor with Jackie, Vicki, Linda and their kids. I approach a crater where the bathroom knob hit against the wall, the door's ajar. An officer's footprint stamps in the fear of them coming back—his voice still booming, "Next time we'll take your children away"—and I go never mind.

**At four years old, I hide behind the door** to the bedroom I shared with my siblings. Painted royal blue and I see all the ways my cousin was too heavy with the paint. We are living in a two-bedroom apartment on Fulton Street in Brooklyn.

Gerald comes for a visit, which will be his last, and it is just me and my mother in the apartment. The place is clean. Frankincense burning, Pine-Sol-mopped floors, and this royal blue I've cornered myself in—maybe Gerald will not find me here.

He doesn't know the floor plan, how I find comfort in closets, in corners where I do not punish myself but pray. Pray where I am the quietest conversation with myself.

But Gerald finds me. Calling my name lures me from believing I am an island. Pulls me across waters so indigo there is no bottom. Welcomes me on a shore that slips and slips from under me until my feet trust again.

I hear him loud and clear:

> "Why you runnin from me?
> I am your father."

> My feet resign.

> Father isn't a place from which I can run.

**Some mornings Bing takes an interest** in my life, in my schooling, and wants me to perform my tricks. "Say your ABCs" is this morning's request. I start off perfect and then LMNOP, which I recite as a jumble of sound, makes my stepfather furious.

His Guyanese accent always created distance in me, between us. Instantly in sound we're foreign to each other and I have to tune myself sharper to catch him. His tone and those "eh, eh, ehs" schupsing like a rock skip, skip, skipping then striking my forehead.

Over his dreadlocks, King Selassie looks right past me. Everyone at the table, mother too, my brother just a toddler, but his stare observes tensions, my pulling away. I don't want to be there. Bing seeing me for letters I cannot produce.

I begin again, arriving sloppily at LMNOP, and for the third time, I refuse to go past C. My body refuses. My tongue is tied. It is not safe here. I can't understand the mountain in his voice. Why deny me Farina and lemongrass tea? Why am I a *Stupid, stupid girl!*?

**Those bangles were Guyanese gold,** my mother recollects. Still bothered that I, as a first grader, ignore her instructions not to take them off, and set the pair of bangles inside my desk. Each chime, my teacher stops dead in her writing on the blackboard or looks up from her desk to notice me. Her look turns me red-handed. Each time I move, this bright gold jingle undermines the control she has over us. Our silence is a sign of obedience and respect. She is known for being a disciplinarian: quick to lessen you with an outdated insult like Don't be a bump on a log. Or stupid is as stupid does. Or outright pops you on the back of your head with her pencil. Or gets in your face and yells herself flush. Because nobody needs such noise, I toss the bangles in a trash pile on our way to the cafeteria. When I come home, wrists free, I tell my mother, "They fell off."

**"What is wrong with you?"** My mother wants to know. She carries me into the 79th Precinct. I was testing how far I could click in the handcuffs without them locking. Going for the thrill of escaping by the skin of my teeth. I was successful before, but when they locked, they were tight around my ankles. Shuffled and hopped and the bobby pin or fork or Philips head couldn't do the job. The metal dug to my bones.

She lifts me onto the front desk, three tiers high, and the officer asks, "How did she access an official pair of NYPD-issued handcuffs?" My mother kept them in the dresser's top drawer—my older brother said she and Bing got freaky with these. So her response is a lie, a whole lie, and nothing but a lie, and we aren't freed from the officer's judgment.

**I got on a sunshine yellow tank top** in the second grade, and by midday, a kid's footprint is an emblem on my chest. I threw a chair first. It misses his head by this-much. He says, having seen me in C-Town paying with food stamps, I'm on welfare because I have no daddy. Now everyone is laughing at me. For something I have no control over. For the love that commits my mother to my care. He has no idea who I am. My punishment "for starting the fight, young lady" is to sit in front of the classroom with my desk to the board and practice my cursive. The word is "ship." I write it on slant, the "p" becomes "t," and I'm spelling "shit"—five times for muscle memory.

> The red ball-
> point draws
> my attention,
>
> correct
> these
> 'ships.

**"Gerald gave you your first and middle names."** My mother shares this with me each time I ask about its meaning. Especially the first name others insert an additional "s" into and pronounce me wrong. Who is this Arisa without a souvenir mug or key chain?

"He came up with it." She speaks into my hair as she parts and combs it. "I wanted to name you Melissa."

Not what I need to complete my homework assignment—this disappointment in her. Every Melissa I knew was Puerto Rican and was, at some point, sent home from school for having lice. This is the first time I am grateful for my father. I ask her again.

She divines its meaning and I feel her body pause:

"Precious Jewels."

**Third grade ended and summer vacation started three days ago.**
My oldest brother says I keep saying his name over and over
again. I think back on that overcast June morning when the car
hits me, I can't remember my voice coming out. My brother
says, my orange goes up and falls down in slow motion. Briefly,
a crystalline thread connects my left eye with the right eye of the
driver. We give permission to fear. There is dampened darkness
that leads a procession of filmic clips: EMT cuts my aquamarine
Jordache stirrups. Neighbors seeing me—that boy from the
fourth floor we sometimes played with. The woman from the
sixth, always with a headscarf, who looks like the actress Lynn
Thigpen. All of them in states of O. The chill cubic containment
of the ambulance. My mother's face blanched with worry, all her
color recedes so she can be stoic. Bing, deep umber with tears.
Dreadlocks stuffed tall in a knitted cap, he looks Seussian. His one-
winged questions     "Is she OK?     Is she OK?     She OK?

      She OK?"        fall like manly snowflakes to muffle beeps,
sirens, tires on speed, and all our panic making angels in the snow.

**I broke my ankle and damaged my liver.** Scars on my face from skidding on asphalt. I was in and out of consciousness the first night. Everybody comes to see me those two weeks in Wyckoff Hospital. They come with sesame candies, cherries, fried chicken, and bubbles of little plastic toys from the twenty-five cent machines. Granny, great aunts and aunts, uncle, cousins of the first, second, and third degree. Friends of the family who go way back and laugh from an exclusive place when they say, "Remember when . . ." Everybody from my mother's side visits, and Aunt Lulu's caution of "Cross on the green and not in between" makes no sense.

**I believe in God, I talk to myself.**
I sometimes sing from the fourth floor
of our apartment into a sky as starlit
as it was going to get in Brooklyn.
Fifth grade, my voice on cruise as Rose Royce:

> *I'm wishin' on a star*
>
> *to follow where you are*
>
> *I'm wishin' on a dream*
>
> *to follow what it means . . .*

And my neighbors holler back, "Shut the fuck up!"

They weren't ready for this songbird.

**Scotch bonnets of the highest alerts**
rubbed on my left thumb while asleep.
Their anticipation wakes me,
performance added to their morning routines.
Will I or will I not put it in my mouth?
      dish soap
      Tiger balm
      nail polish top coat—
Poison Me Right wasn't a name by Avon
but it tasted that way.

Soothing worry anxiety fear, the skin
chapped and pickled from daily triggers,
calms hunger into a good girl,
which means I don't thirst for oil.
Rusted with insecurity and ponder,
my teeth are not of their concern—

my brother shoved me with the quintet of years
between us, during an afternoon of horsing around,
my front tooth chipped on the concrete floor.
Its jagged edge is over a year old and rotting—
it is their embarrassment they need to solve.

I'm too big for this thumb and therefore must burn.
But there is something too little that requires it to stay.

**Hide-and-Seek is my favorite game** because you must come find me to become a winner. We've been hanging out with Linda's kids, Jamilah and Marcus, on the weekends. It's a Saturday, our moms gone out, and left us in the apartment to our own devices. Jamilah and I decide to hide under my mother's platform bed, in a tight corner. She's in front and I'm behind her. The curve of her butt sits nicely on the top of my thighs. And my body notices what is nice about it. I start with a subtle hump, guised as an adjustment to better hide myself. My oldest brother is counting and one hundred is near. I do it again, explain that my feet are sticking out. The sweet throb in my panty needs a few more humps to bring it to death. I don't ask Jamilah's permission or consider her pleasure, and she starts yelling "Stop, Stop doing that! Stop," and I am tagged It.

**My brother doesn't know he has a bag of empty crack vials** in his coat pocket. It falls out, while walking late to his figure drawing class, he thinks it's a sandwich bag of Swedish fish. Candy of the innocent kind. The history teacher picks it up—"Excuse me, young man"—and he is sent to the principal's office. My mother has to leave her job in downtown Brooklyn and go to the high school in midtown Manhattan. What yarn she spins gets my brother no suspension.     But Bing.          She knows it was Bing.

**Out of habit, we keep the kitchen light on for Bing** so he can see his way into the apartment when we've all gone to bed. Instead of his keys unlocking, my mother's drowsy feet, door chain in its track, the switch and lights off. Not even a week, we soon realize: Bing's got a change of address.

**I don't remember this,** but my mother says I bumped into Gerald on Nostrand Avenue. I am soon to graduate elementary school. My memory, musk and incense. The weather, kerchiefs flagging in pockets, antennae clearing waves. She says this happened, but what I hear, Gerald's unhello moving southbound with traffic. Where he stood, concrete and haunt of curry. Knock-off handbags, bootleg videos. Not a beard or brow, style of shirt, he could be anybody.

**My mother wants to know what I think.** I think the ring doesn't properly fit her finger. That cluster of diamond flecks is dull and dirty. Its round shape makes her hand mannish. She's considering her new boyfriend's proposal, and I'm amplifying a *No*, this time spoken by my spleen. "Cornell is Jamaican and hardworking and owns his own mechanic shop," she says, and it's good for us to have a father. Even though this one's given her a black eye already. We are at Granny's house for that weekend while she gets herself together. My oldest brother and I in the bathroom talking about what we would do to him if we had might or money. Now she's admiring possibilities on her hand.

**We can't have nice things,** and somehow we, the children, are to blame. We live mismatched. Stuff rarely organized. Stuff thrown in plastic bins, large tote bags. The dressers are hand-me-downs handed down. The wood rails, nubs and dust. The bottom of the drawers fell out. The closet doors are off the tracks. There are no hangers to hang things. No shoe racks for all our shoes. No privacy, either, since Bing ripped the bedroom door from its hinges to remind us we are spectacle. And it was five of us—one adult (sometimes two) and four kids, living stylish in a two-bedroom apartment.

I want things to have a place where they can be easily found, instead of rummaging through the "sock bag" to find the match. Or in that garbage bag in the back of the closet. Or someone is wearing the only belt that goes with my outfit. I start sleeping with my clothes, school uniform, and accessories folded at the end of my bed. I need a clear demarcation between what is mine and what is yours.

When my mother tells us we are moving to a larger apartment— three bedrooms in a duplex and my oldest brother decided to live with Granny—I figure more space would mean nice things. But Cornell is moving in with us.

When I see my new bedroom, the rainbow wallpaper my mother and him hung up, the center panel is upside down. The rainbow is wrung and breathless. My headboard jangles and my sister's bed—we all know she is prone to bouncing and heavy-bodied— collapses by the second week.

The mechanic has no sense for fixing things, except for cars and me interfering on him beating my mother. For which he rips the poorly assembled headboard from its screw holes and threatens to "Fix me proper." My mother stands there exhausted, and my vulnerability is confirmed.

I pay a fee to the male
for my passage through this doorway—
enter as girl, leave as other.

**I play hooky and study the subway map.** Veins of trains moving below and above the Big Apple. A way to get to every borough, Long and Governors Islands, too, and that's not counting bus lines. This city wants us to circulate.

I love taking the F to the last stop. Watch people. Watch the light change on our faces when we go from Carroll to Smith-9 Streets. Regardless of the time of day, the world opens up, and we better flex our glow. I look out the window at rooftops, the geometry of streets, telephone wire, to what's beyond. Let my body jostle with the train's momentum. Excited by the sight of the Wonder Wheel, I stand to exit minutes before the train comes to a stop.

Stillwell is salt and heavy-aired. The exit, shadowy and damp sleaze, especially during the off-season. Cross the street to Nathan's to get a hot dog with extra 'kraut. Get myself a bag of bluepinkyellow cotton candy and head to the boardwalk. A biker rides over unattached boards and it's xylophonic. The wind, wind, wind and my feet sink in and out of sand.

I finish the famous hot dog staring at a buoy going back and forth like a drowning man. Take a Bic pen from my book bag, drag it along the wet sand, and the ocean follows in and then dissolves the groove. I touch the ballpoint to the tip of my tongue, imagine a blue beauty mark there, and swallow it whole.

Sit on a clean patch of beach, watch horizon and waves, and write on repeat, *My mother will not marry Cornell My mother will not marry Cornell My mother will not marry Cornell My mother will not marry Cornell My mother will not marry Cornell My mother will not marry Cornell My mother will not marry Cornell My mother will not marry Cornell My mother will not marry Cornell My mother will not marry Cornell My mother will not marry Cornell My mother will not marry Cornell My mother will not marry Cornell My mother will not*

*marry Cornell My mother will not marry Cornell My mother will not*
*marry Cornell My mother will not marry Cornell My mother will not*
*marry Cornell My mother will not marry Cornell My mother will not*
*marry Cornell My mother will not marry Cornell My mother will not*
*marry Cornell My mother will not marry Cornell My mother will not*
*marry Cornell My mother will not marry Cornell My mother will not*
*marry Cornell My mother will not marry Cornell My mother will not*
*marry Cornell My mother will not marry Cornell My mother will not*
*marry Cornell My mother will not marry Cornell My mother will not*
*marry Cornell My mother will not marry Cornell*

until it is true.

**Friends never really ask about fathers.** To ask is to sometimes signal a personal failure. But when we feel triumphant from figuring out how to play handball with all three of us, it comes up.

Nicole with her round cheeks, dimples dipping into them, undoes and then meticulously fastens the Velcro straps on her Reebok classics,

> "I often wonder
>
> I wonder but
>
> I wonder most
>
> I become a homing signal,
> an umbilical cord
>
> My father, a rum zero,
> will never add
> my expectations my deepest needs
> and the years divide us"

She pauses and turns and looks at me and Safiya, our backs against the handball wall. I am watching for that ultramarine sky that marks when I need to be home. Nicole's eyes are asking,

> "Is my father some kind of dream
>    reeking of crazy and Old Spice—
>    simply a distance in everything?"

Maybe we nod. We nod soft so she knows it's not her fault he never came back home from the liquor store.

Safiya, whose father lives with his other family in Harlem, rolls
her eyes, neck, sucks her teeth, inspects her hot-pink polish,
bites off a hangnail, then spits,

> "He's nothing but
>
> a warm brown set of limbs
>
> never thinking
>
> never knowing
>
> the appropriate measuring tool
>
> to sift his love from them to me"

They clock me for my story, with a silent impatience of thirteen-
year-olds feeling fresh from sharing, and the sky is telling me to
go. I rise up, dust the street off me, and the blood flows to the
pin-and-needles,

> "What?!
>
> I never had a father
>
> I figured you might know"

We laugh something purple from our throats:
it rushes forward with many rivers, freely and deep,
muddy, and ready for the open.

**I leave girlhood**
and enter my own
private world.

It is eighth grade, pleased my white denim Gap
jeans went unstained, I put my sweater on,
cross into new territory.

No decipherable shift: sniff-sniff,
ten fingers and toes, crackle in my ankle
remains, and now I'm fresh dirt.

For which I take for my own making
into a woman whose shoulders cup
over her heart, head bowed, convex
my cramps turn me. Smoldering fire
churns my uterus, perineum, stomach
to switchblades and Chinese stars.

It takes my mettle to breathe, stand up, sip, because waves
of pain, tsunamic.    Advil    Aleve    codeine    Vicodin
oxycodone are prescriptions to drown.
                    In tears, passed out on stairs,
moaning fetal in my bed, because it occurred monthly, my
family disables their care. My anger toward them, a sail. I
get into a raft, away from where it hurts most. A black-sand
island covered by mist that thins and thickens from can't to
can't. No one sees me from the distances taken from "female
troubles," "her time of the month." Left on my own nausea,
mouth watering itself, and out it gushes. I dry heave myself
to sore.

On a scale of one to ten, the pain of my wandering womb
is blue violet. This does not compare to the blue black of
Africans, according to my mother. Her period was never
this bad. My blood forges through walls, seeps out a quarry
of pomegranite, heated and fine, setting things apart with
its edges. When I'm this kind of lunatic, my endometriosis
casting me in its spell, I must stay away from the water. A
whispered command of *Come to me* makes the Hudson River
the boats.

> Spawns joy so spontaneous a girl
> takes off her shoes, rolls up her
> pants, jumps into a university
> fountain, turns water conga, conga
> her body wet, sings the moon into
> her mouth, then kisses me, wane to
> full, at my dorm door.

I don't need to abandon my body to feeling unloved. I find
antonyms to past verbs.

> I fall leagues
> for a girl
> whose long
> red lava she ties
> into a bun,
> rubs a balm
> of raspberry leaf,
> cramp bark,
> motherwort and her
> honest heat
> onto my belly
> lower back
> ankles,

I cry.

Pain bristles
across softcover spines,
throbs toward
the languid mist
outside my windows
where she
secretly watches me
when I'm writing,
then tiptoes through
my apartment
bringing New
England brisk,
granny tonics,
and pirated DVDs.

Every month
she calls in sick
when pain notates
power lines,
warble and evensong
through horsetails
to a brand new
honeymoon—
she holds
my pain
like a newborn
beast in her hands
and coos it down.

# II.

"The moon runs until the day catches it."
—Guyanese proverb

**On a visit to my mother in New Jersey** from the Bay Area, where I lived post graduate school, she takes a long good look at me. She's transported. Updating her visual, taking stock of what she saw last against what's now.

Her eyes treasure a find:

> "You have Gerald's hands.
>
> Your feet are his, too."

I pull my hands and feet closer to where we belong.

> "And that way you draw people to you," she says, "that's his charm."

**I have a Shango dream**—Yoruba god of fire, lightning,
and thunder, depicted with a double axe. A white and red
wedding—I wear red Converses, a monarch train, my arms
free of fathers.

> Bing's sister told me to be careful
> not to "sweep dem feet" as a young
> girl. "You wanna not get married?"
> I swept the floor, swept every love-
> child inch of my body from the
> "ting" my mother chased.

Truth be told, under certain weather, a young girl becomes
a weak woman. Cloudy heart, spine partly, I felt the
pressure of an adult front. Proposed, three different times,
drunk, to the same ex—I couldn't vow to a blade that knew
my insides soft—

> I'm already of split definition.

**I'm not sorry for my one-way streets,** my way or the highway, manly waters incompatible with my sex

Swear by my cocksure shine, don't believe one person can give you all that you need, polyamory is the way to burnish

I'm not your daddy  Will not top you to stay  You are your own bottom

"I work at pleasing me      Cause I can't please you and that's why I do what I do" —Erykah Badu

I'm not trying to be *in* love, I'm searching for a new preposition

Discerning and cautious about who gets close to me, my trust is earned

Love is a verb and is space and not asking me where I am going all the time

I panic at the knowledge of my own real existence —Bernadette Mayer

My attachments are to memories, lightbulbs, cardstock, dreams— immaterial drops of golden sun

Let's remain under the spell of objectification

Once the chase is done, I eat the sweet thang

Unconditional love is a boat that has sailed—conditions now apply

From home to globe, I know the extremes of people—my hate is a soluble line

I take all sides, shape-shift, my moods and language mutable, too slippery for words and evaluation

I am used to being unaffected and misrepresented. I live short and fine as the doll most nestled. My bathwater is nobody's business, my complaints squeakless.                    I burp and, goddamn, Gerald is noisome and stinky

**I break a woman's heart for reasons not-her-but-me,** for feeling romantically incompetent, for guilt that her needs do not matter to me          She is better off

Oh, she keens—a city of sound born from split metal and a felled mountain. The ripping reveals a network of rebar never to hold earth again

She weeps a river, valleys wet. Babbles, creeks, and baggage. Sobs mistfully north to south. It is clear where we end now, and she is rushing far, then farther

                    pushing out her banks, making sure
                    the flora and fauna damns my name.

**Romantic    Intimate    Others are Rios**    rivers reflecting
rivers eroding my edges
rivers running and rivers drying, shudders

A Rio-before confluxes with the Rio-after—
rivers opening up my heart
for me to see

**These fatherless Rios** I love make themselves lost-to-be-found. Objects for the daily, keys and wallets, agendas and phones, they can't find their things. Seriously. Her stuff in nooks, spread and sprawled, commands attention, requires care. Irks me finding her glasses on her head, credit card in the jacket worn the night before, nail file on the table where she left it, notebook right there. They don't get stressed out, neck tight, and shallow breath to look for what's mine.

**I never ask these rivers,** *Where's my father?*

**I walk with a poet friend around Lake Merritt,** all its miles, starting from the east and then returning east. The hour holds us in amber. I say to my friend, "I'm ready to be a woman who's matured her femininity, who appreciates all that has gotten me through, that has gotten me here." A grown-ass woman not subdued by shame, I set forth. Several double-crested cormorants surface from a deep dive in the lake's brackish waters. Their wings spread to dry and geese fly in arrowhead formation.

**The Rio I'm dating at the time** invites me to a potluck brunch at an old Victorian, in need of a power washing, near Old Oakland. Inside, the furnishings make me feel like I'm back in Fort Greene, Brooklyn, 1996 to '98, late summers when the heat warmed our tones. I laugh with some of the poetry people I see out at readings, Santigold sings from a Bose, my Rio goes for a cinnamon bun, I visit the lush garden out back. Turquoise tiles pathway through tomatoes, lettuce, chard, string beans, lavender, chamomile, fennel. I pull a sprig of mint and when I stand, there is her athletic build, strong teeth, her smile, she extends her hand and introduces herself as "Mondayway—Mondayway Flores. I live here." Asks if I want to try some of her latest honey.

**Here, at my feet, a gift basket.** Thought it was the mailman, but I answer the doorbell and find no one but a pair of flamboyant artichoke blossoms. Two large organic yams, flecked with earth, chamomile and mint—redolent. Rose Moon honey, a lavender satchel, and a kraft jewelry box—inside, a circular fishing sinker on a fourteen-inch gold chain. Nice. The card reads, *Queen, the only thing not from my garden is the gold and you.* A heart is drawn with a crown, signed *Monduywuy.* I gather up the gift before any neighbor witnesses me betray my commitments and smell her lavender.

There are some rivers that flood over man-made embankments, because they hold a memory of a wild prior, of an unrenovated before.

*"Nobody ever told you,*

     *all you must hold on to*

          *is you is you is you"* —Erykah Badu

I say "Fuck" soft enough to not disturb my shame. The blood from my finger turns the water pink. I'm cutting fatherlessly. I can no longer deny that's how missing begins—attention on so many things, I show up in fractions, then divisions, and no one ever sees me. It's a challenge. I'm in a situation and what I do is offer a maze that bobs and weaves a new style whenever there's a demand to love one-only. And Mondayway is Aqua Net.

**My heart swollen sad shifts me into a strange shape,** I excuse myself from public. The city doesn't have the same charisma anymore. Was told never make your friends choose. No one chose me. No one called. I'm so thirsty, I drink an entire birthday. So lonely, I knit a cave. I fear I may run into old friends and fall into old rivers.

I'm talking to my boss one afternoon and to my surprise, I say, "I am lonely." There is no metaphor between me and lonely. I've been putting people between me and lonely. Said I'm in love to send lonely away. I've been achieving and succeeding and I'm still paying off student loans and being a literary citizen, a second-class citizen, and, once, regarded as nobody at all. I'm lonely.

So quiet and lonely, I masturbate next to me sleeping, I never wake. I take extra time rubbing shea butter on my feet, legs, hips and ass, slow dance solo to "Guava Jelly." Who else to love me tall, steward my desire? Who else to grease my scalp, braid rows of corn and cane that map my beauty and liberty?

Mondayway wants me to account for my shadow. Wants to know why I'm not _____. She sees what I am doing as insufficient information. Her operations interrogate the negative. But I'm here, looking behind me, and lonely. Someone come hug me.

My mother said, "You raise your daughters and love your sons." Gave me her face and said to herself, "Who's going to take care of you?" Testing if I've absorbed her logics, her belief, *If there's a will, there's a way.*

I've been laying will and making-do
and we knew this growing up
black girls and hand-clapping:

*Trying to make a dollar*
*out of fifteen cents—she missed*
*she missed, she missed like this*

and we made Xs and Os
with our arms and legs so we
remembered to hug and kiss ourselves

I cheated to hug myself blue in the face.

I haunt my studio apartment. Aggrieved when you put the
pieces back together, scars look crueler than the original
stitch. What used to be a treat for Fridays and Saturdays,
every hour now a 4:20. I take bong hits like my last breath,
my only breath, just to keep breathing.

**I stand in the coat-check line** to get my jacket and get the fuck out of the club. Mondayway is heated. Found my slow whine with a man vulgar. My view, the guy had moves and was a tall memory in which I could escape. His cologne, a breeze of body water. The bossa nova synced our bodies to a rhythm uncolonizable. No borders between us, his curves like sea beneath me. We wind and blend our selves like horizon, and finally I was coming up for air.

For each syllable, Mondayway's finger jabs my chest, a stream of "Fuck   Bitch   Slut   You want to suck his dick like your thumb?" and then she spits on me. It lands on my jeans, right thigh. The jeans, distressed and black, and her spit makes a darker stain. I take Mondayway's marking in no nonviolent way. See a history of racism and lose it. Fight hard until bouncers separate me from her, tell me to take my coat and go.

Into the chill. An early-morning night, I'm in shock and shaking. I pick up my pace, pick it up some more, the lights in the master's house were never off· My breath goes in burning, comes out rough. My body lost to the same old fault lines. I run from Mondayway's fire. Run to outrun the body's invention. I stop beneath the lake's necklace of lights to vomit. I failed in what I loved and what I didn't love.


Where am I to go?

## i apologize*

she apologizes

i see us

at our emotional age

we are fresh initiates to hurt

we are shriveled adults

we pull light inward

we're dim from too little sleep

tossing through harm I've caused

disgusted how dare she spit on me

red flags, counting regrets

i don't hug her   i step back

allow our scar to begin.

---

* "I'm sorry" is spoken into hearts that are within the heart, with flexible volume to fit between the wounds' lips, which appear closer to shut the father I go. We trust the darker-dark.

**My therapist says,** "We attract the people who are going to help us heal what we came to heal in this lifetime."

It is convenient for Mondayway to label me the cheater and not claim her role—the one willing to pursue another in a relationship, to court with jewelry and time. This is the cruelty of her honesty. She doesn't reveal herself in the process. Doesn't allow her vulnerability to be here with me. She doesn't care for my dignity, for the presence of esteem. In her assessment of my character—so causal and very little spiral. She's asking for a death, but she is no wake to celebrate its homegoing. More executioner than I'm willing to offer my neck.

I exist within a cosmology of experiences. Her critiques, supported by her routines, standards, and worldview, volleying between two poles of right and wrong that don't serve no body. Causing harm and founts of resentment. There's a soluble line between love and hate.

Without dignity, I am naked before a crowd. I reinstate walls to defend. Without dignity, I can't hear another's truth. My body is tuned to the ring-shout of voices saying, *You're the beauty your ancestors dreamed.* I self-preserve—I don't show mine, if you don't show yours.

Our desires are made in our entire image. I fooled myself into expecting my desire to take a shape holier than I. Come to find out, every grown-ass woman has her grown-ass girl. Mondayway occasions what default behavior looks like—it is so unkind and unloving to yourself and others because you've subsumed an authentic part of yourself to activate it. Reduced the other person to some triggering trope and so both parties go missing in the exchange.

I see this in myself now.

**I could have killed her**—old she I was, she I sometimes wish I could be, she who didn't know better, didn't voice and protest, she who doesn't hold herself in the confidence I hold all others.

I'm negative-below in myself. A heart's shaking where my fist used to be. Anger needs someone, someone not loving me.

I stare into Lake Merritt and welcome returning to water. Not those fitful instances when tears are running, snot, and spit reminding me of my elemental kinship, but the deep Sankofa longing to go back and get what I've forgotten.

Trying to put strength in my voice and convince myself I'm more than—what?!—I speak to a dear friend. She hears my walls breaking. Says, "Arisa, it's OK to be human."

Human?            How to be human when conditioned not to be.

Confusion takes the thought of walking into oncoming traffic from my feet.                              I go home instead.

**My therapist says I've gone from an open field**, a complete clearing where earth pauses from making anything tall, to a seed encased in its shell. Our love is a tight squeeze. I disappear by implosion to feel that clearing between the forests of my worlds.

I've lost the beauty I've imagined for myself in her critical gaze. My mercurial wit, ludic ways, erotic fire and ice, the sure is given over to the plea. *Please see that I am a parallel truth. Please take care in how you choose to speak to me.* I don't know how to ask for this.

My therapist says, "What is loving about this relationship with Mondayway is your courage to rescue yourselves from being subsumed."

Bringing light to the dark, dark to light, I attract a person who calls checkmate. "Queen, let your heart break." Who deals in the invariable facts and energetics of the body. How it's showing up, here and now. How it feels. What it needs. And the depth and quality of my body's relationship to itself and others. Wants me to care about these things, to be present and live new stories—imagine how good that could be.

Mondayway says in a voicemail, "You can't forgive me until you get inside your heart and grow."

**At the darkest hour, there is no demand to show,** to dissemble, to give, I unhook my breasts to spill to gravity, sink into the bath. Orange blossoms stick to my skin like mother's kisses and overdue apologies. The peppermint soap mentholates and constellates my anterior stars go through the Florida water to shine. Deep breaths open my tight chest, and I feel how running has taken more than given. I rub my heart with the heel of my palm, and my heart stays voicing,

> *Find your father*
> *Find what's missing there*
> *Find what is enough*
> *Find yourself whole*
> *Forgive and be forgiven*

# III.

"Woman rain is never done."
—Guyanese proverb

**My mother says she has an address in Guyana.**

"You want to write your father."

It is through inflection she makes her directives questions.
She doesn't intonate high, just enough so her implicit meaning
isn't lost to freedom of personal choice.

> I feel my face
> up against the bluest door
> and it's about to open.

**It was Avery, Gerald's youngest brother,** who gave my mother the address when she ran into him in Brooklyn one weekend. I meet Avery over the phone. This is my uncle. He lives in Queens, NY, he has a son, my cousin, and I'm branching out in ways that make me anxious. I'm thinking more people to be accountable to, more expectations to navigate, more care to give. His voice is commanding when he calls me ARISE. Says it in all capital letters. Reminds me of the direction I must go.

Avery tells me Gerald has many children, maybe ten, and he's been trying to unite us, help us get to know his family. My family. I'm unsure and hesitant. Feel overwhelmed and say, "When I'm ready I will." At some point in our short conversation, he informs me we are descendants from a maroon colony in Venezuela. Later he emails me a list of names and birthdates that include half-brothers and half-sisters; uncles and aunts, some living in places like Tennessee and Arizona; one uncle died in the late 1970s; Gerald is a Leo; his mother recently passed—my grandmother. And my grandfather is dead, too. Died when Gerald was eleven years old.

**I'm not invited** to know much about my father's family because the family is concerned I'll write about them. Avery told me this. They keep the black-boy magic from me. My father's family bequeathed what Gerald started: in the tenth year of his life he wrapped his words mute. These words are tight-lipped cowries I pitch to the ground just to get inside. They keep the black-boy magic from me. It's an unexplored complement that is active and I do not know its properties. Throws me off-kilter, like one leg is shorter than the other and caught in a whirlpool. I have a gangster swagger. My stressed foot, dipping      dipping      dipping      and turning up wet.

**I find and friend another Gerald-child on Facebook.** My Facebook Sister, who is by nature half my sister, but nothing nurtured these halves. She went to my high school, three years after I graduated from the High School of Economics and Finance. In one message, she has very little to say about Gerald. Near nil information to give. "I wasn't checking for him like that." She has no longing to know her father. She is soon to have a child and takes selfies that show her baby bump.

**I find and friend a second Gerald-child on Facebook.** My Facebook Brother, who is by nature half my brother, but nothing nurtured these halves, is five years younger. In a series of messages, we set up a phone call. Bryce tells me Gerald was deported for battering his daughter's boyfriend. This boyfriend was beating her. Attempting to kill her. Was there a gun—my Facebook Brother doesn't know but Gerald was charged with a felony. For this third strike, he was sent back home to Guyana. And I envy my half-sister for that moment she felt her boyfriend topple from her, relief from abuse, and she entered the cove of Gerald's care.

**I'm noticing, lately, fathers with daughters.** Of the pictures my mother gave me, I don't have a proper portrait of Gerald—so much chiaroscuro, not enough good. The Polaroid sends cracks through his face. His dark skin absorbs all the light and features aren't distinct. The windows into his soul are shadowed. I'm on his shoulders; we stand tall as the buildings in the distance. My toddler-face squints at the sunlight. Neither one of us is really seeing.

**My mother gave me a dirt road,** a house in a township with a tin roof that makes music from all things fallen, in a country of many waters, where the man whose sea-nymph surname represents the beauty and bounty of the sea. I write my father at this address.

**Dear Gerald,**

I am Denise's daughter, and this is the dream I had of you: The sky ingratiates the sea and is as blue as it desires—this is the backdrop as a car drives us down a natural road, flatlands and wind-cleared. Before us, a city glints, your right nostril comes into view—a fine-etched keloid web, I touch and something is lit in me. Your irises pitch black and a mouthfeel silence where a bond used to be.

Do you remember I bear the name you conjured, its attention turned to your shorelines, to the father missing in us both? I was born on the cusp of fish and fire, five months after Jonestown, in a county of Kings. I now live with my girlfriend in California, and the state is experiencing a drought. The more I notice, each season brings an extreme. Why weren't you summer?

I watch a housewife on TV tell how, on a visit to her father's, she lost her leg at six to a farm machine. She's beautiful—looks like a horse—but in her head she's missing a leg. Every time she talks you see the image she has of herself. You see how animal she's become and her fear that she doesn't belong. We will see it—her good foot—and wonder why God allowed this to happen. Question, *Where was the father?*

Soon to come. Off performing noble clichés. Little girl I was thought you were love by way of disappearing. I have been a screen for gazing. Allowing the bigger picture to eat the smaller picture; you're one of the classic oldies reeled from my heartbreak. I cheated in my last relationship and my feelings coalesced for you. That girlchild me, full of so much fight and sorrow, is tale-chasing in a scapegoated posture a perfumer would call fecal. I'm tired of feeling like shit, blurred vision from spinning. I cannot see clearly my belonging.

**No, that isn't the actual letter I sent,** that's the poetry. I wrote a formal note, greeted him the same:

*Dear Gerald,*

In the body, I mention my mother, Mondayway, living in the Bay Area, that I'm a poet, an editorial manager at a dance magazine. Said I would like to reconnect and learn more about him, and he about me. Kept it short and simple, fewer than 250 words. This was my initial contact to see if he was still at this address, to know if he was still alive. I signed it:

*With love,*
*Arisa*

And then a postscript: *I would love for you to write me a letter so there's something of yours I can keep.*

Inserted it in an envelope, along with a business card that has my picture on one side, my phone number and email on the other. At the post office, the postal worker at the window tells me she has family in Guyana. I respond, "Me, too!"

**Several weeks passed and on February 14,** I received a call from a strange number, and I let it go to voicemail.      It was Gerald. His accent is aged and grave and so I listen with my whole body. It takes me a few playbacks before I make out all the numbers to his mobile.

I called him back on Skype. The connection is bad. His voice moves through a static cloud as thick as our estrangement. But I heard it and our greetings to each other are joyful.

I place my ear to the computer. His tongue is not mother, it's fatherfast, and it's making me anxious. He recites a poem. I catch every other other other word, and these remain in my hands: "window    identity    down the river."

He gives me the permission to write his poems and therefore mine. Tells me Avery sent him a copy of *Hurrah's Nest*, my first book. Says I have the madness in my poems.      What this madness is?      It is passion.

He spells my first name, says "There are stories in each letter." What those stories are, I can't hear. My name translates to "there is sand" and each unit of sound means "to know when it's enough." This to add to my mother's "Precious Jewels"—a beach and diamond-clarity in knowing an end.

Then for ten seconds the static clears, and without difficulty in understanding, he tells me "The only father you got is God—the only one to cry out to, the only one who can hold your body."

He goes into his yard, in hopes that it may improve the reception. The closer he gets, the bird chirps sharpen and insects come into play. The lull of his patois returning my ears to him. He says into them, "I remember your birthday."

He warns me time is running out on his call, and he leaves me with "I love you, Arisa. I know I wasn't there but the love, for sure, was." Then the static goes dead.

Mondayway says, "What a perfect Valentine's."

**For sure,** no call from him on my birthday. I am out with friends, drinking gin and eating puttanesca, and so no voice message comes as no surprise.

**Gerald calls on June 14.** I'm watching Mexico and Cameroon play in the World Cup with Mondayway.

First thing he tells me is that my brother is coming to visit him.

Because I have four brothers who I was raised with and consider "my brother," I ask, "Which brother?"

He says something sounding like Sha'ron.

I say, "Bryce?"

Gerald wants to know if he's talking to me—Arisa—because I feel incorrect to him. I confirm I am present. Feeling nice on two beers.

He again says, "Sha'ron."

I say, "Bryce." I only know of a Bryce. (Wtf.)

He wants to know why I haven't called.

I want to know why he hasn't written, but I keep it to myself. Give him some context. My life. What I do. Suggesting that the center isn't him.

He wants to know: "What're you getting me for Father's Day?"

The Fucking Gall.

I ask if he's serious and he is. I respond with obese laughter. Laughter eating supersized laughter. Laughter buying bulk. I collect myself, say, "Our relationship has not earned gift-giving holidays."

(Quiet.) Sounds like he's in a public place. Voices soft patter in a dull nightlife ambience.

His feelings are hurt. I ask if he's OK.

"I'm cool." He says, "Cool."

"Are you really cool?"

"I'm good, man."

I do not prod any further, and,     "So     I     guess     this     is good     night     ?"

He gets off the phone, but doesn't turn it off properly, and I listen to him curse me. His teeth-sucking cuts the air. And I hear it, so cutlass and bright,                    "Bomboclot"

**Look how quickly, my entry through that doorway**—daughter
turns to blood cloth, to menstrual pad, to toilet paper, to rotten,
evil-smelling decomposition.

An expletive used when surprised or vexed.

My father figures me obscenely. Breaks my heart along
the same fault lines that ache for him. Like fathers before
who want my pudendum as wound as offense as trigger
to freeze me in a female pose—hands up and legs apart,
full-stop, period.

In my right to remain silent, I'm not literal.
I'm not a force of nature.
My blood clots and does not run on.

**What is my spiritual condition?** I go from numb to wonder. Mondayway's framed by the window, streetlight haloes her head, crescent moon in the upper right pane, an exponent to her temple. I sit between her legs to get my hair done. The combing, then pomade, the massage over my scalp—she lifts my skull, stretches my stem, and my marooned thick hair, she plaits fishtail. Once completed, Mondayway serves me a glass of welcome. Says, "Swim."

**First, there is sand.** My body moves across the rough translation of my name. The sandbar's coarse gravel on my feet is pressure in my lungs—expanding to hold a maiden volume of resurrection. The surf washes me of the terms by which I've been assembled on land. I don't see the plunge coming. I find myself deep and salted, waterwalking the league that holds me buoyant. I feel the residents of ocean, great and grand, the way it is one teardrop gigantic, and God—the MotherFather of them all—speaks to me:

> It is that rebel pearl-diver blood who makes you other
> than what is expected. It is Negra Azalea, Venezuelan born,
> beneath shade of trees that scream their hurt when roots
> are torn, Isla de las Lagrímas. She is the woman who planted
> your freedom. She's the tierra that features most.

Without words, Who I am? is answered

> You are that depth of sea survived. . . .
> When a MotherFather says ship, a MotherFather means
> the one from Dutch— Prima Madre in its belly,
> learning ways she is flesh around a seed.
> Azalea in her womb. When We say ship,
> We mean Prima was. Shipped
> then shipped, she didn't know where she was.

Without question, I know where I am bound

> She wanted for her daughter swimming ways.
> Cape Verde, her island, taught her so.

*Prima slaved for pearls. Carried down*
*into feet by boulders, Prima's body greased,*
*a slick allegiance to finding Negra Paca's black pearl—*
*in a league she couldn't quite descend, in the mouth*
*of a diver named Paca was Prima's freedom. The pearl*
*the size of your eye, and many lost sight getting to it.*

*What emerged from Prima's darkest deep*
*wasn't the jewel of another's suffering, but home*
*she tasted too frequently in these waters. She blacked out,*
*gave up her air for the drink of it, and rested.*

A blueblack darkness guides me forward, and I am following Azalea following Prima. A glowing trinity of albino manta rays light where Paca drowned. The black pearl set in her mouth.

> I come from
> Azalea's lips:
> that kiss
> that takes
> the pearl.

**I'm congratulated by the Center for Cultural Innovation.** Awarded a grant, in which I promised to write and self-publish a book of epistles about my father's absence, then go to Guyana, meet Gerald, give him the book, and I once prayed for this but the humid conditions between my palms have changed. I feel all tines and timid about now having to meet the man and not the Wiz. I inform those closest to me and my undergraduate professor, Ogunyemi, writes, "This will be good for your spiritual growth . . . a well-tended garden of azaleas."

# III.

"A boat which has gone
to the waterfall cannot return."
—Guyanese proverb

**We go to Guyana during the wet season.**

Sitting at the gate at JFK, I survey the people—Do I look like I'm Guyanese? Do I look like the country?

Guyana is highly Christian, then Hindu, followed by Muslim, and buggery gets you ten years imprisonment. It's fascinating, the need to legally protect assholes. From an internet search, I read that singer-activist Nhojj is raising funds to build a LGBTQ+ center in Guyana. In any case, Mondayway and I think of our husband stories while we wait for the plane to board.

**Flying in, we see the Guiana Shield,** dense tropical rainforest covering Guyana, Suriname, and parts of Venezuela and Brazil. From above, heads of broccoli; the Atlantic Ocean, a pensive indigo; the Demerara River, black tea sweetened with condensed milk. We land and the heat is a heavy touch and our driver is waiting for us. I see so many Indo-Guyanese on the roadside and I'm matching myself in color, seeing where I fall on the Guyanese spectrum. There are billboards that say "I am Guyanese," with various hues to illustrate this country's history: Amerindian, Dutch, African, British, Portuguese, Indian, Chinese. Everyone here has so much sun in them. So much sun. We pass by towns with the names Friendship and Herstelling. For a five-minute stretch, the smell of sweet porcine shit follows us. The driver says, "That's coming from the rum factories."

**We arrive at the Herdmanston Hotel in the Queenstown** neighborhood of Georgetown. The receptionist checks us in, introduces herself as Edna, with formal diction that makes me want to correct my posture. She tells us this is the best time to visit because "We will be celebrating 'Mash'—Mashramani," Guyana's Republic Day. Since 1970, when Guyana became a republic, Mash has been held on the anniversary of the Berbice Revolt of 1763, the largest anti-colonial resistance effort by enslaved Africans. On February 23rd, everybody comes out to dance, eat, drink, watch the decorated floats and costumed revelers parade on by. The hotel is a block away from where all the excitement will happen. We thank Edna for communicating this information we read about in our traveler's guide. When we get to our room, I call Gerald several times and the phone keeps going to voicemail.

I've come this far, and he knows I'm coming this far. We spoke two weeks ago. I'm worried and embarrassed we will not meet. Mondayway and I go to dinner and she's hopeful he'll answer tomorrow.

# DIFGHDIFG
DIFGHDIFG
Do I For Give Him Do I For Give

What if the question, *What is forgiveness?* is my own need to solicit an apology? To put a mouth and throat and all the systems that make a body talk onto something I cannot touch? So it can give me sound that bounces off my contours, that let me know I'm here. A living beat.

What if forgiveness is a matter of breaking up syllables then arranging the word with a whole new set of feet.

What if, *Can you forgive him?* is a means to end the contrast, is a way to ask for our bodies to be proximal. In that asking, I'm proposing that a knowledgeable skill exists, that maybe all the tools we need become real through use.

What if this protected reality I made with imagination is let-go, and with the release, I've accepted wildness? The proverb says that it's better to have one bird in hand instead of two in the bush. The release will leave me birdless.

What if The Father isn't The Answer and I've been seeing it all wrong. There is an unequivocal honesty to Gerald's absence—it is reliable and transparent and hasn't done or said otherwise. Can't I see that?

What I know is that absence breeds madness, an irreconcilable relationship you know is there but can't call it by its name, can't leave it because it's a tree with its root collar breathing around your neck.

What if poetry is how I practice my relationship with my whole body—bodies unknown and not yet born, bodies past, future bodies, bodies present. The father and mother of my poems are two pearls I nacre at any point in time.

**It's the second day in Georgetown,** and I have called and called and Gerald hasn't answered, hasn't returned my call, and in the first voicemail I left the hotel's address, number, and now I cannot leave a voicemail. This doesn't feel good. Mondayway keeps the spirits good and we go for a walk and I'm trying to be present but the sadness is a pillar in my chest, marble and anguish. My tears do kaleidoscopic things to my sight. I walk into the street, and the traffic moves by British rules, the minivan comes so very close. The hood's hot breath on my hip. Mondayway pulls me fast onto the sidewalk.

We walk toward the Sea Wall. The town is feral with discarded water bottles. Plastic bottles, plastic bags, plastic junk that can't decompose. The area around the Sea Wall is trashy, the sewage too strong, the Atlantic coming in brown and sandy. Me and Mondayway wonder why there isn't a beach, some beachside bar to sit and drink a goddamn Banks. We walk down Albert Street to return to Herdmanston, and we share with Edna our observations. She tells us that Guyana exports sand. Beautiful white sand. But it's the politics that keep the country from developing.

**"'Sacrifice zones' are the places of social abandonment** where Americans are trapped in interminable cycles of poverty, powerlessness, and hopelessness as a direct result of changeable policies that enforce capitalistic greed and allow individuals, families, communities, and ecosystems to all be 'destroyed for quarterly profit.'" —Henry A. Giroux, *The Violence of Organized Forgetting*

Am I a site of abandonment?

Now cite the person who has abandoned you: Gerald says, "The only father you got is God—the only one to cry out to, the only one who can hold your body."

He has abandoned his part.
He has abandoned himself.
He has abandoned his semen.
He has left the pudendum.

A few months before this trip, I put out a call for letters because I was curious to know who else—who else plays that guessing game of *Is That Him* or *Where Is He*. Eighteen letters, far as the Philippines, some from inmates in San Quentin, and poets from the Bay Area, written to fathers, to absent fathers, estranged and dead fathers, to their retreating back, to that space left in their wake.

These letters lighthouse the kinship of our suffering, our similar wanting, how we extend in the world and cannot explain that whole note, in a state of O, but never saying.

Dear, A man who wasn't there
anthony lee porchia
Raffy

Dad
American G.I. No. 1
father
Floyd
Robert
Tennyson
Whoever You Are
My Father
Dad/Dennis
James Keith
Sperm Donor
Who is Jeffery?
Mister Midget Man
My dear Pops
Ben

At one point, I thought to answer these letters and do the work
the fathers couldn't or wouldn't do. But that's not my name.

**Mondayway and I are sitting down having Banks beer with sorrel,** and a woman comes to our table and introduces herself as Osvena—my father's cousin.  *My father's cousin?*  She tells me that my mother called her aunt and her aunt called her and how did this happen?

Yesterday, before we went on our walk around Georgetown, Mondayway messaged my mother on Facebook, and I think, *This is so sweet of her.* My mother then put a call-out to all her Guyanese connections. And just when I'm about to ask Osvena where is my father, I see a six-foot plus, dark-skinned man swaggering toward our table, black slacks on, white short-sleeve shirt with the first three buttons unbuttoned, a breeze giving view of his pecs, a red kerchief tied around his neck. This must be Gerald.

With all his pride, stars, and planets, he sits next to me at the table. I give him a hug and his returning embrace has the self-consciousness of a teenage boy. "For truth, you're the spitting image of Denise," he says with conviction like no one has ever told me this.

The waitress comes and Gerald orders himself a Banks. I find it odd he's not saying hello to his cousin. I comment on this, and Gerald responds that she's not related to him. Osvena remains steadfast that she is *my father's* cousin. I'm confused. There is a moment of awkward silence, Gerald's arms fold against his chest, he says, "She can't have two fathers."

I have a flashback of Bing: he walks toward us in his blue prison coveralls—his skin lacks the luster sun gives you. He approaches like a muted siege of rain clouds. Desert and melancholic, he offered up a lake when he saw us there. And now, I have no eyes for what's become of him.

Osvena is Bing's cousin. Bing is in Guyana now, living in the bush, doing mining work. Osvena hasn't heard from him in nearly six months. We have some bland chit chat about Mash, our thoughts of Georgetown so far, and when we tell them we walked down Albert Street, Gerald tells us he used to live in Alberttown growing up. Soon Osvena finishes her Banks and gives me her number to contact her if we want to do anything fun for Mash.

Once Osvena's out of earshot, Gerald sucks his teeth, repeats "Your father," emphasizing *your* and shaking his head. I ask why he's so ruffled by this. He tells us that my mother married his rival—Bing. "How is she going to raise my child with my rival?" He sucks his teeth again. I'm seeing that my mother was scandalous. This is some Capulets and Montagues shit—Bing and Gerald in rival drug gangs back in Brooklyn. Gerald got sent to Rikers and some prison down south in the 1980s and '90s as a result. He says, "It's good I wasn't there."

We order dinner. I notice how old Gerald is, his eyes turning cloudy blue. He complains the salt fish is no good; it tastes like shark, and if he was living in a proper place he would treat me to better. He shares that there is a tradition: the daughter, upon arriving back home, prepares her father dinner. I look at Mondayway and roll my eyes and chuckle, and say, "Isn't it tradition for you to provide me with the kitchen, pots, and food to cook?" He lets out a baritone cackle, dismisses me with a wave. I tell him dinner is on me.

His Creole is thick and I do my best to catch his words. Something about Denise being his first love in the States, even though he was married to another woman at the time. From that marriage there is another Arisa, born on my same birthday. I eye Mondayway to make sure I'm hearing this right, and she confirms I'm hearing this right. He met my mother trying to find his way around Brooklyn, 1977, and he bumped into her on Fulton Street. Pure accident and chance. He keeps on saying he loved her, between forkfuls of food that does not meet his taste.

Gerald savors his earlier days in Georgetown, pointing where a tall building once stood, recollecting on how he charmed women from their spouses, rubbed shoulders with the political elite as a detective on the police force. Soon the sky is night and I'm taking in as much of his stories that I can hold: his family's wealth and how he grew up tossing his clothes on the floor and there were maids. He slows down his talk because the hurt is deep down. He foresaw the death of his father who was lashed in the head and thrown in the river two days after Gerald broke muteness to report the dream that portended this calamity. He never got to rest his eyes on his father for one last time. Never got to see him buried. He was eleven years old when he died. Gerald's dream frightened some family members, caused a rift in relations, because they thought he possessed an evil darkness.

To this day, coupled with his reckless ways and criminal activity, his relationship to his kin is strained and distant. Now sixty-six years old, his toothless grin is mischievous and adolescent when he confesses, "I've been a bad man."

Before Gerald goes, Mondayway takes a picture of us. I am happy and happy to give him money for carfare and his mobile bill. I later look at the photos on Mondayway's iPad and map the similarities of our bodies. She says we have the same hands and stature. But I don't know when Gerald was seen as no good. Seen as up to no good. Where is nothing good about him? And what good is he?

**"In the wake,** the past that is not past reappears, always, to rupture the present."—Christina Sharpe, *In the Wake: On Blackness and Being*

Is his father drowning the original text of our suffering? The root of my father's amnesia and erasure of himself as father? What is the medicine for that?

The waves are urgent here. Everywhere in these waters the drowned grandfather resides. Was he brought to the Demerara River? Hands and feet tied? His body beaten against the water; he like cans strung to a newlywed's car. Was it money or a woman who took him down? What did he know or do to be given death by water?

This is the old man fortune-tellers have seen. Three different tellers, in three different states, said, "An old man is with you."

Everywhere in these waters the drowned grandfather resides and Guyana is the "land of many waters."

**20 February 2015**
Georgetown, Guyana

Who is my daddy? A fallen bourgeoisie nigga.* Who crossed boundaries, he moved through the world like everything was his own. I'm sure he rarely heard no, and when he did, conflict. In part, he blames the systems for excluding him from my life and for not allowing him to live at his standard.

Deported to Guyana eight years ago and on his own reconnaissance, he admits it was his involvement in an attempted murder that got him sent back home. His daughter Tiffany— Gerald said he knew she would bring him trouble—had a knife to a man's side and Gerald said, "Oh, no." He took the fall for it and chose Guyana instead of correction.

---

* I say nigga invoking grown women, kin and fictive, whose company kept and grew me. There is a chorus of agreement that commits nigga to the page. The "er" has been dropped, and Gerald has emerged from the rooms of the master's house with nothing to show for his time, except unsociability, self-absorption, and virility—these black excesses of masculinity with no substance to give it credence. As a nigga, he has returned to the mother tongue—the long "a" sound that survives in "Ma"—because this is how we reclaim and recover ourselves when the emergency room ("er") has no science for making the spirit well, for setting the spirit on a healing path, for putting you in right relationship.

**The next day, Mondayway and I go down to breakfast.** I head to the bathroom, and upon exiting the facilities, there is Edna. She asks how it was meeting my father, "Did you have any nightmares?" She's grinning with equal parts teeth and shade. Joyfully, I tell her, "No nightmares at all." But after sharing this with Mondayway, I feel the jab of Edna's insinuation. The stigma of her gaze. We have a slow-eating breakfast, enjoying the heat and bake.

We return to the room and I Skype my mother to thank her for putting out the bat-call and the mini-drama it caused. I tell her that Gerald said it was good he wasn't there—in my life—and I agree with him. I'm meeting the creator of such absence and I have real eyes for the man. Before getting off the call, she recounts the dream she had last night of Gerald.

It is his birthday and he's getting dressed to celebrate. An electric blue suit with an orange shirt and a bow tie. She says he looks good in the suit and, in the dream, I comment about understanding her attraction to him. But in the dream, "Gerald's shoes are mashed up and he walks on the heels of them like a crackhead." He puts so much cologne on this fabulous suit it stains. To stop him from spraying, my mother takes the bottle and warns me against such overindulgences.

**"When you represent something** you're basically creating a counterfeit for something that you think exists." —Meleko Mokgosi

I'm representing Gerald in this way. Sitting and talking to him is like putting my money down, betting I can find the queen of hearts. The whole time, the queen won't be revealed, not from his sleeve, not in front of my eyes—absent is the most valued royal. Absent are the favors in my odds.

A fast talk. A talk slippery as silt. A talk that can lay the kinks down for a minute before they recover and find their spring. A talk all bounce and booty booty booty booty booty booty bounce on the floor, up and bounce booty, your eyes sweat. Mouth drops open and it's hot in here. Humid and elusive is this booty talk, filled with pirates and parrots and peg legs and cross & bones, and another's man treasure is another's man treasure, even if the talk is fool's gold

Is it okay to say, *This is enough*? I got what I wanted. My once fatherful self. She who didn't fear a significant one leaving—that frayed, mute feel of disconnection. She who knew the presence of father, knew his there.

> I got her back,
> who I abandoned
> in his going.
> And, *Yes,*
> *she is enough.*

**It is Masharami.** The music started blasting at 7AM. Reggae, calypso, soca, chutney, hip-hop. And people are finding their way to the parade route. It's not even noon and it is hot. I'm underwhelmed. The West Indian Day Parade in Brooklyn had better floats. Mondayway points out that the cultural politics of conservatism unravel with all the whining, grinding, and booty shaking. I can easily hold what appears to be a contradiction. It's all that water in the body; ocean waves residing in marrow, and when the wiggle is unleashed, as Big Freedia says, it is mimicking currents, turning back or moving forward time. Generating a spiral motion to collapse boundaries between spiritual and material, to restore us to our polyrhythmic accordance with life. It's a route to freedom that can easily appear wild and uncivilized to eyes trained to harness the body's energy for its own entitlement. On this day, the whole country (re)members their independence, ancestors who resisted enslavement, because we don't get free by straight and narrow and abiding by the master's comportment. The same speakers that woke us up play shanto into midnight.

**24 February 2015**
Georgetown, Guyana

We go to the Guyana Zoo and the animals are kept in small cages. The otter swims diagonally back and forth in its pool; the puma, ocelot, and tiger prowl ten steps forward, then ten steps back, giving the funkiest stink-eye to rival the odor coming from their cages; the monkeys are so vexed and tired of being spectacle they toss food at us and shake their cages in the hopes that this time the bars will concede.

Adjacent to the Zoo are the Botanical Gardens, which are simply manicured lawns. Stretches. And Mondayway and I wonder why don't they expand the Zoo into the "Gardens," or give the animals to a nature reserve and stop maintaining this inhumane colonial pastime. This is what the whole colonial enterprise does to the living—structures and contains so our living serves the system. These structures are centipedes in our heads, bodies, and psyches—a madness that then precipitates the need to separate from ourselves.

The "Gardens" make us hungry. On our tourist map of Georgetown, the Cara Lodge is advertised as a hotel and restaurant, serving cocktails and authentic Guyanese cuisine. On our walk-about, Mondayway takes photos of old wooden doors, weathered from sun, rain, and those salty breezes coming from the Atlantic. The old churches look the most like ghosts—white paint peeling, shuttered windows, their steeples moan with mockingbirds and pigeons. We see a man, possibly in his 30s, with a deep gash across his head, lying unconscious in the sun, his calloused feet in a puddle that a stray dog laps. Should we do something? We follow the example of students in cobalt uniforms who pass by and treat the gashed man like nothing new.

We walk in rectangles and squares to find Cara Lodge and when we follow the direction in which people's fingers point, still lost. We hail a taxi and the driver takes us to a block we passed twice. Cara Lodge is tucked into the street, out of view, a cathedral of palm trees at its entrance. The hostess welcomes us. Escorts us to seats in the garden area, and while giving us our menus she asks if I am Guyanese. I reply, "No." She goes to put in our rum punch orders and Mondayway says, "Yes, you are. You are Guyanese American."

I would be more willing to claim the Guyanese if I were reared with the culture. Bing wanted to be Jamaican. The only thing Guyanese about me is my father and we know how that goes. Gerald is caught up in a past-time, a heyday, the glory days and there's no place for me in that. All the "what-ifs" and "remember-whens" make him unavailable to me. He has made very little effort toward my life.

Guyana is abandonment from my father. I feel the weight of the people in me and I in them, guilt I carry myself alone. Feel survival or selfishness, *we can do without you* and it's familial. We got stuff between us—stuff we don't even know. Their faces are my father's face and I am bereft. I wonder, where do I belong and will I ever?

I come back to now, to heart, to being present in my breath, I breathe, I breathe, I breathe because no place or no single person or people is belonging for me. Without anger or desperation or aspirations to be zen or enlightened—I get it. I get how much I needed others to belong to me, to *be-long*—to extend over a considerable length of time. To be a solid-something to return to and name myself alongside, to identify with in hopes that it will confirm the future. That I will not be left and therefore will not need to face my own ideological, psychological, or physical death.

Similar to how Gerald wishes for constancy of what was—if government gave him his pension, if family gave him his inheritance, if he was paid what was owed, then he could truly live. But searching for the constant orients life toward *having* and not *being*. Spirit is restless in a state of having, and I'm not having that. I'm being a legit motherfather to myself.

I order the Metemgee with fried fish—a traditional dish with African origins. In Twi, "metem" means plantains, and "gye" means to delight, and it's made with a selection of local ground provisions slow-cooked in coconut milk and topped with fried fish. I could eat Metemgee for the rest of my life.

**An outlier,** I come from outright liars.
Fathers and mothers, long lines stand out.
Rule breakers, deadbeats, and beaten dead,
those who make-do and sou-sou,
pool stones and stew stars.

Bodies come into lightburst—
lay limp, shell shards around them.
Those encaged, weasel in stink and shit,
nowhere to run, spine can't tall.

Here on margins, bread buttered
with margarine and cow ceremoniously killed.
No gin turns tongues to truth.
I am your sweaty faces, proud to put elbow
grease in pepperpot. We upper-crust lineage.

We're trust thrown in the eye, dust
kicked up roadside and carried home,
we strip off our skin to burn again. From stolen
and drowned hands, we earned that daring to cross.

                    Our phantom parts
                    and foot-in-mouths,
                    we pastiche appliqué
                    moaning to be
                    our own story.

**After a late breakfast,** Mondayway and I are sitting on hotel grounds smoking cigarettes and the wind is good and cooling. Raindrops start out innocent, then come devilish down. Heavy and cold, it leaves our skin goose-fleshed. We return to our room and listen to the thunder hush us. The lightning shocks us. Clouds are thick and today we experience gray, all things cast in gray. Nothing dualistic in thinking, thoughts come from the middle.

I read in the *Guyana Times* about an eighteen-year-old male who was drugged and raped by a gang of ten older men on Old Year's Night, December 31, 2014, in West Bank Demerara. After the incident, the eighteen-year-old went to his sister's home and told her what happened and then he went speechless. He managed to identify three men, whom he knew and worked with, but he's unable to give a written statement. His mother says he's traumatized. "Every time he see a car coming in he direction, he run in the house and collect a cutlass as if somebody coming to do he something." His mother hopes when the statement is provided justice will be served.

Will justice ever be what love looks like in public? Where we are transformed by its presence, its courage and bravery, to live by its own alphabet.

Gerald's private voicing of apology and love released me from making backwards apologies. "I love you" brought me forward. Brought this thing that is there and not there into a broader relationship. I arrived from coital secrecy into daylight's crude legitimacy. Embraced my shadow and it spoke in a voice solid and reverb, and I heard I am tangible, whole, and visible by heart.

**25 February 2015**
Georgetown, Guyana

Everything is wet. It's been storming, and I've seen Gerald once so far. I haven't met any additional family. It's how Gerald was in Brooklyn when I was in Brooklyn—we rarely saw each other. Similar still, this is our way of relating and being with each other.

Who's your daddy?

A portrait of absence and presence. A story, a tale, told in a patchwork fashion. A composite of estranged fathers. A knot of deadbeats, wannabes, has-beens, what-ifs, can't-shows, and so broken. Assembly is required, no batteries included, and to this I laugh wolf and jokerish. I eat him. Chew Gerald down to marrow and shit him out for dung beetles. A life incorporated.

**"In its potent ability to decree that what is is not,** as in a human ceasing to be and becoming an object, a thing or chattel, the law approaches the realm of magic and religion. . . . [There is a] fundamental human impulse to make meaning from phenomena around us. . . ." —M. NourbeSe Philip, *Zong!*

Or from what is not around us. What if no meaning is made. I let the absence be absence, nothing more. The relationship is to the "not." We relate to the not. Learn to be with all things not there.

*Why are you not here? Where is my*_____? has been asked for generations. These echoes populate the absence and silence of where they once were or are supposed to be. There's no contact between human beings that does not affect them both.

*Where have they gone?* is an anthem in the body, a political dirge, keening from our mitochondria.

**We have two more days in Guyana,** and the rain stops in the early afternoon, and we take a taxi to Stabroek Market. The driver lets us out, says, "Be careful," and we enter a hive of activity. I nearly have a panic attack. There's all kinds of honking going on. Honking to alert pedestrians. Honking to advertise that this taxi or minivan is available for passengers. Honking from driver to driver as greeting. Minibuses, sedans, army-size trucks, with drivers who think their cars are people. A yellow car nudges me on my right thigh to encourage me along.

There are catcalls. One asshole wants to know if we need a cab and I wave a No and say "No" as well, and he goes on to say something about my height and then shouts, "You don't like short men. Short men the best, you know." I ignore him still, and he threateningly tells me to watch myself. Mondayway is catcalled "fit." She looks at me in confusion, wanting to know what that means, and I'm like, *C'mon, boo.* It doesn't take much imagination to know what it means when a male grazes upon a female's body, athletic, young, old, in her prime, prepubescent, or adolescent, he's sexually assessing her, constructing how her body will fit the need of his body. I say, "Ready, prepared, ripe, strong—you got the stamina to work the fuck out."

We can't brave the crowd that appears to be inside or around the Stabroek Market, so we locate a sports bar before the rain comes down hard again. We ask the bartender where we can go to buy gold jewelry. We drink for two rounds before the rain lets up. We get a taxi to the bartender's recommendation and arrive at an establishment with an armed guard out front. We say hello and he allows us through the first locked door. Then we are buzzed into the main store where vibrant Guyanese gold shimmers in display cases.

All the pieces I want are too expensive for my two-hundred-dollar budget. Mondayway finds a basic 10-inch gold necklace and hinged-hoop earrings. I convince her to let me buy the necklace for her—after we banter back and forth like two market women—as a thank-you for being with me on this trip. For helping me to recognize that there are all these brilliant women in my life, herself included, who uplift me more than my father could. And she, wanting me to have some Guyanese gold, insists that she buy me the earrings. I try them on and they are perfect. I keep the earrings on and she wears her necklace, too, and this makes us feel safe when the guard opens the door and returns us to submerged streets.

**Water-dead is how Gerald killed us.** Dead as in no function. Water-dead as in with no marker, no grave, rest-less. Restless and repetitious in memory, we are not at rest.

Is his father drowning the original text of our suffering? The root of my father's amnesia and erasure of himself as father? What is the medicine for never to have seen your father buried?

Where you "remain" is not known. You do not remain anywhere known, you're haunting. You inhabit the living, and you remain restless and repetitious within us.

**It's our last full day in Guyana and we wake at 5AM** to go to Kaieteur Falls. Kaieteur is the longest single-drop waterfall in the world, with a total distance from top to bottom of 822 feet. We fly in a nine-passenger airplane that was built in the 1970s. There are ashtrays for us to deposit our butts, and at one point, the aircraft hits turbulence and drops half a mile in altitude. I grab Mondayway's hand in preparation for our death. The world we fly over is rainforest-occupied, rivers, and then it opens up into a gorge and mist abounds.

We land and the air is so fresh it's like drinking water. We take a moderate hike to the top of the falls, and while on the trail, our guide tells us to stop, turn to our right, and about eight feet away is a cock-of-the-rock. A rare bright orange bird with a crescent-shaped hairstyle. Our guide tells us we are lucky, because people come here from all over the world to see it and go home disappointed.

I'm in awe. Before I knew the legend, there was the impulse to let the water take me down. To fall with it, to give into its seductive forceful tresses. This is what the Patamona Amerindian chief named Kai did. Sacrificed himself to the Great Spirit Makonaima to save his tribe from the Caribs. He took his canoe and paddled over the point where the Potaro River plunges into the gorge below. "Teur" means "falls" in the local dialect. It's believed Kai remains living in a cave behind the drop and when mist surrounds the falls, Kai is cooking. Possibly a meal, I wonder, to welcome his daughter home.

I get myself as close to the cliff's edge as I can muster, to see the depth, to feel the pull of earth opening up. I run my hands in river water, pick up stones of that hard red-black rock we stand on. Lay prone on it, press my breasts  belly  hips  thighs,  turn my head to the side and listen. The rock is warm and it vibrates. Its touch resounds, shifts my molecules to resemble its molecules and I'm unlocked and revived by a wild   sacrificial   grand   love.

**We meet up again with Gerald, one last time, for dinner,** and he takes us to a roadside eatery called Spicy Dish in Alberttown. Walking there, I notice Gerald constantly adjusts his crotch, grabs at his cock and balls to make sure the jewels haven't been stolen. He's flapping his mouth. Me and Mondayway are there to give the illusion his monologue is a dialogue. He's talking to affirm that he is somebody, that he does exist, and that his existence needs my care. Sponsorship back to the States; shoes size thirteen; pants: thirty-three waist and thirty-six inseam; a nice watch; ten-speed bicycle; twenty dollars a month for rent.

I lost my full-time editorial management job six months ago and I've been collecting unemployment to supplement my adjunct teaching. The IRS sent me a letter four months ago saying I owe thirty-five hundred in back taxes, and if it wasn't for this grant from the Center for Cultural Innovation, I wouldn't be on this trip. Gerald hasn't asked me how I pay my monthly expenses, those credit cards and student loans that have me in $80K of debt, how I stay financially afloat in one of the States' most expensive cities. When I got that bill from the IRS, I kicked a hole into the kitchen cabinet because I was stressed-out from operating in the negative. Then I was pissed at myself because it will cost money to repair the cabinet door. Did he ever wonder, *How is this child of mine being clothed, fed, sheltered, and educated for all these years? How can I contribute? How can I help Arisa?*

I asked Gerald, during one of our phone conversations, for one thing, and that was to write me a letter. I wanted something tangible from him, something I could return to again. He said, "No, my handwriting's no good."

At Spicy Dish, I put in an order of saltfish and bake; Mondayway gets chicken curry; and Gerald requests oxtails, even though the server tells him twice, "We run out." He's schupsing in disappointment about how this is not a proper restaurant because they can't keep plenty of oxtails. We sit outside with our Banks, and I'm already exhausted from listening to him. From his manipulations that turn you into an object for his purposes. It's incredible; I would never think to ask someone to financially care for me when I have no functional relationship to them. Patriarchally, I get his reasons for this entitlement to the fruits of my labor, because he *gave* me life. But that transaction was between him and my mother. He and she benefited the most from the activities of each other's bodies—the givings their bodies gave.

The other reason for this trip: to give Gerald a book of epistolary poems I addressed to him. The poems were my way to gather the courage and words to write him an actual letter. He looks at the cover of the book and says, "Who's this?"

I thought it was a picture of him, according to my mother.

"This is not me. I don't know who that is."

And I laugh—of course it's not him. Why would a book of poems addressed to my estranged father have a photo of him on it. And since the Polaroid was worn by time and handling, I'm guessing the picture is of me and my Uncle Butchie, who Gerald very much favors. Butchie passed in 1988. In the photo, I'm sitting on his shoulders. Although one male can biologically be my father, the work of loving and tending to my well-being was done by brothers.

Our food comes out, as well as the neighborhood dogs, and Gerald remains miffed by the reality his absence created. Waving the book to punctuate his speech, he says, "That last book of yours," referring to *Hurrah's Nest*, "you dogged out Denise." I'm trying to reconnect to the love I felt in Kaieteur Falls because Gerald is getting my goat.

*What the fuck do you know!* is headlined on my brow. My frustration is without exhalation. My disappointment, a lacuna. What has he built to bring us close?

It's no secret, we evolve our stories with the ones closest to us. With the ones who remain. Bless them, they bear the brunt. They take, and give, blows and blows meant for others. They take more than they deserve. Give more than asked. I'm grateful my mother's body rings and rings and troubles her when I'm not near. Her intention is to be present in the best ways she knows how. From her children she gets what she needs to soul repair and examine hard truths invoked by our presence.

I watch Gerald, on my last night in Georgetown, relish in trying to find a fault line in my relationship with her, and it is plain to see this sixty-six-year-old man has nothing but an opinion and no muscles for love.

**"Love is a skill.** To love is to have the willingness to interpret someone's on-the-surface, not-very-appealing, behavior in order to find more benevolent reasons why [those behaviors] may be unfolding. To love is to apply charity and generosity of interpretation." —Alain de Botton

Am I the dog now?
Am I the dog, dogging?

The bitch who slides up to Mondayway with a request in her eyes? Her ribs and sagging teats. Mondayway gives rice and peas, chicken, and the dog eats, then goes away. And why is there not a specific name for a male dog? The bitch has returned with her mate and Mondayway feeds them both.

Gerald laughs and I see his remaining teeth. He says, "It's her fair skin—her 'Porcheegee.'" Connects Mondayway's generosity to race. I'm shaking my whole black heart at you, Gerald.

You got it wrong. I am the bitch, Gerald. And you—not I—dogged out Denise.

**Gerald walks Mondayway and me back to Herdmanston** and I give him one hundred dollars and carfare. Mondayway offers him a decent bud of marijuana that we brought from Cali but can't take back with us. He says, "Yeah, man, nice." Wishes us a safe flight, and we hug goodbye. His embrace, sure and reassuring. This has been a long day for Mondayway and me. Tired from our adventures to the Falls, we get to the hotel room, pack our bags, collapse into bed, and drift asleep watching *Big Freedia*.

**The moon, bright and ocular, wakes me.** The translucent curtains fail to block it. I go to the bathroom and my period has come. Heading back to bed, I hear the Atlantic. It is like Kaieteur Falls in my body,

*D I F G H D I F G*

*D I F G H D I F G*

*D I F G H D I F G*

A cock-of-the-rock on the balcony's ledge asks me, *Do you forgive him?* But it is as silent as a traffic cone, the speaking is inside of me. Mondayway is knocked out snoring and I go to the glass door, part the curtains, and the bird turns from profile to portrait, and asks me again, *Do you forgive him?*

My body answers by lighting up its beauty marks. My pinky, shoulder, knee, cheek, ear, my panty glow because there's one at the start of my upper thigh, bridge of my foot, between my breasts, forearm, and I step onto the balcony to get closer to the cock-of-the-rock and it flies away. Lands on a tamarind tree across from Herdmanston. It repeats the question, and my body responds by casting light upward, matching me to the stars. In my left view, in the distance where the Atlantic is cresting and crashing, another set of light-strings shine down, the way dew dapples a web and you know it's there. The cock-of-the-rock says, *Keep walking forward*, above treetops, phone wires, no people out, and wind sweeping the streets. I'm one step at a time, imagining a tightrope between me and those strings of lights. I relax into my natural gait, and wonder, *What's this conjunction I'm on?* And the bird responds, *Forgiveness.*

When it came to the conjunction "and" I was illiterate. For it makes you larger, more. Expands into distances beyond my eyes. It coordinated in my throat left feet, knobbed-knee mortar.

It expressed itself like a stiffening gurgle and all my sound was shamed, stopped. "And" made no sense to me. It is alien as "A" turning "I"—but should we not see the first letter of our name in I? I could not give "and" my tongue. Have it used to "connect more than two elements together in a chain." Whose body is linking itself to me?

Just beyond the Sea Wall, I see the silhouette of my father's body against the dark urgent waters, and wind overcomes our sound. My feet meet sand. Gerald is kneeling on a water lily. To the right and left of him, petals hold a pile of bones. His eyes are missing eyes, instead an atmosphere of speckled vanta-darkness, swirls of dense gray clouds. In each hand, a black pearl. His stare is directed toward the horizon where the day will break. His voice finds me, says, "I, for truth, loved Denise," and that is the living thing between us. Wet with his tears, his face shape shifts from young to old: from the old man I know, to the face my mother loved, to the boy waiting for his father. The cock-of-the-rock tells me, *Then he will rest.*

This is the meal I'm to fix for my father. The feast for his eyes is his own father's face. With his tears, I wash Gerald's hands and feet, which are my own hands and feet. I collect the pile of bones, leaving two bones behind. Grab a discarded plastic bottle and confront the water. I feed the Atlantic twelve bones, and each time a bone strikes the surface and descends, my uterus feels the discomfort of discharging. The surf encircles my ankles in foam while I gather the ocean in the bottle. Although just a liter in volume, it holds the gravitas of answers, unspoken. Since my heart is strongest, I carry the bottle in my left hand.

Starting east, I pour a circle around Gerald. His feet turned skyward, the constellation of beauty marks on his soles is bright in the night. We are where we're supposed to be. Looking like an inverted seven, ebony and complete, Gerald becomes an island surrounded by his father's salt.

I close my eyes and read the Atlantic for my grandfather. Opulent blue. Dendrites resurrected. Ballots and chains. Shadow agreements. Shocking leagues. Sugar cane and black-eyed peas. Seashore and rum shots, waves aggress. A mountain moves before my eyes, and the wind delivers Gerald's voice to me, "My mother said he never come home."

This negative is my grand-absence before my life began. Like eighty thousand river-gallons making one single drop in me, I say,

> ARISE
> GERALD BASTIAN NEREID
> MY FATHER WHO IS YOUR NAMESAKE
> HEAR ME TOO—THIS IS ENOUGH
> I AM WATER, I AM FISH
> I AM DAUGHTER OF NEREID
> AND YOU AND I ARE I AND I
> WE ARE STARS AND I, STARGATE
>
> FATHERS BE RESCUED FROM A TOXIC MASC(ULINITY)
>
> YOU'VE FED YOURSELF TO A SYSTEM
> CAUGHT NO FISH, NOT A YUCCA TO BOIL
> PLANTAIN STILL UNPICKED
> YOUR CHROMOSOME, A SHRIVELED OFFERING
> YOUR HUNT HAS NOT MET OUR HUNGER—
> WHO ARE YOU FODDER FOR?
>
> FATHERS BE RESCUED

YOU'VE ABANDONED LOYALTY TO THE MOTHER
HAVE DIVIDED US TO THE LAST NERVE
HAVE DISTRIBUTED OUR POWER AMONGST YOURSELVES
HAVE LOST CONNECTION TO EARTH WHEN YOU LEFT
YOUR SERPENTINE SIGNATURE IN SAND

FATHERS BE RESCUED
YOUR HUNT HAS NOT MET OUR HUNGER

The Atlantic responds with an ovation of bioluminescence. When
it dies down, I expand my father's circle. Sit butterfly alongside
him in the infinity I've drawn. Inhale the Atlantic's ichor until
my solar plexus is lit, booty anchored, exhale my crown to shine.
I chant,

L M N O P    L M N O P
LUMIN  O P   LUMIN  O P
LIGHT OPEN
LIGHT OPEN

The stars rearrange, our strings intertwine, and the cock-of-the-
rock snatches the pearls from Gerald's hands. Flies spiral around
the macramé of our lights, and as it ascends in altitude, our stars
make the father's face. We look up and Gerald sees Gerald.

From old to young: the graying man I met in Georgetown this
week falls supine onto the sand and I place a bone on his chest;
the charming twenty-something my mother loved falls supine
onto the sand and I place a bone on his chest; and the boy who
waited for fifty-five years to see his father closes his eyes and falls
into a man.

**On the way to the airport, a sign announces the Town of Pearl.**
I interlace my fingers with Mondayway's and I hold on to that
feeling of and. A young man crosses the street with a cart full
of pineapples. Once, and maybe somewhere still, seafaring men
impaled fresh pineapples on their porch railings to let us all
know that the man of the house has returned home, come give
him a visit. I remember my mother saying I was conceived in
the backseat of Gerald's Cadillac, parked on Pineapple Avenue in
Brooklyn Heights. The car, perfectly suited his status—ice cream
paint job and a cherry or two. Said he was too sweet and red
Spanish pleasant, Gerald put the ladies-man charm in the genes.
After a long time away from his arms, he gave her a hospitable
welcome—fresh I-love-yous, her path showered with rose petals,
four-star dinner, divine gentlemannery. She could not wait to get
in the interior of his Cadillac, golden like a natal queen.

# Notes

Page 9: Prologue: dialogue composed from Denise White's letter addressed to her father, "Dear Dad/Dennis."

Pages 10, 42, 66, 89: Victorine Grannum-Solomon, *Proverbial Wisdom From Guyana* (Dorrance Pub Co, 1998), 9; 24; 41; 50.

Page 25: Rose Royce, "Wishing On A Star." *In Full Bloom*, Whitfield Records, WH3074, 1977, LP.

Page 33: "We can't have nice things": Tressie McMillan Cottom, "Black Girlhood, Interrupted," in *Thick: And Other Essays* (New York: The New Press, 2019), 188.

Page 36: "I often wonder.": dialogue composed from Mateo Cruz's unpublished poem "The Math of the Story."

Pages 36–37: "Is my father some kind of dream": dialogue composed from ShaiLynn K. Davis's "A Letter to My Father."

Page 37: "What?!": dialogue composed from Anastacia-Reneé Tolbert's unpublished epistolary poem "dear anthony lee porchia."

Page 47: Erykah Badu, "Apple Tree." *Baduizm*, Kedar Records, UD 53027, 1997, compact disc.

Page 47: Bernadette Mayer's poem "The Way to Keep Going in Antarctica," Poetry Foundation. https://www.poetryfoundation. org/poems/49723/the-way-to-keep-going-in-antarctica.

Page 56: Erykah Badu, "Bag Lady." *Mama's Gun*, Motown Records, 012 153 259-2, 2000, compact disc.

Page 59: "I stand in the coat-check line": Audre Lorde, "The Master's Tools Will Never Dismantle the Master's House" in *Sister Outsider: Essays & Speeches* (Toronto: Crossing Press, 2007), 110–114.

Page 85: "First, there is sand.": Tiffany Lethabo King, "Introduction: The Black Shoals," in *The Black Shoals: Offshore Formations of Black and Native Studies* (Durham: Duke University Press, 2019), 4.

Pages 85–86: Molly Wash, "Enslaved Pearl Divers in the Sixteenth Century Caribbean," *Slavery & Abolition: A Journal of Slave and Post-Slave Studies* 31, no.3 (2010) 345–362.

Pages 92–93: Kirk Smock, *Guyana, Second Edition* (United Kingdom: Bradt Travel Guides, 2011), 21; 24–25.

Page 97: Henry A. Giroux, *The Violence of Organized Forgetting: Thinking Beyond America's Disimagination Machine* (San Francisco: City Lights, 2014), 109.

Page 102: Christina Sharpe, *In the Wake: On Being and Blackness* (Durham: Duke University Press, 2016), 9.

Page 105: Meleko Mokgosi, *The Ease of Fiction*, Museum of the African Diaspora, San Francisco, April–August 2017.

Page 109: "24 February 2015": Eric Fromm, *The Art of Being* (Edinburgh: Constable & Co, 1993), vii–xi.

Page 111: "After a late breakfast,": Cornel West is famously quoted as saying, "Never forget that justice is what love looks like in public." https://www.goodreads.com/author/quotes/6176. Cornel_West.

Pages 113, 116: M. NourbeSe Philip, *Zong!* (Middleton: Wesleyan University Press, 2011), 196; 198.

Page 122: Alaine de Botton, "On Love," filmed July 2016 at the Sydney Opera House, Australia. https://www.youtube.com/watch?v=v-iUHlVazKk.

## Texts of Influence

Dillard, Cynthia B. *Learning to (Re)member the Things We've Learned to Forget: Endarkened Feminisms, Spirituality, and the Sacred Nature of Research and Teaching.* New York: Peter Lang Inc., 2012.

Gillis, John R. "Marginalization of Fatherhood in Western Countries." *Childhood*, 7, no. 2 (2000): 225–238.

Krampe, Edythe M. "When Is the Father Really There?: A Conceptual Reformulation of Father Presence." *Journal of Family Issues* 30, no. 7 (July 2009): 875–897.

Phillips, Rasheedah. *Black Quantum Futurism: Theory & Practice (Volume 1).* Philadelphia: Afrofuturist Affairs, 2015.

# Acknowledgments

Earlier versions of some poems appeared in: *Brooklyn Rail*, March 2020; *HOLD* 2 (2017); *jubilat* 30.5 (2017) *Black Pearl: Eight Poems and a Poetic Drama*, Nomadic Press, (2016); *Origins* 2.1 (2015); *Tarpaulin Sky Magazine* (2015); Finalist for the 2015 Tarpaulin Sky Book Prize; *BOAAT Journal* (2014); *West Trestle Review* (June 2014); *Milvia Street Art and Literary Journal* (2013).

Thank you to the following organizations who supported me with funds, space and time, and audiences: Center for Cultural Innovation: Investing in Artists Grant, Headlands Center for the Arts (AIR), The Daily Grind, Museum of the African Diaspora (Community Voices: Poets Speaks 2017), Goddard College, Mills College, Colby College; and the Hazel Reading Series and Artists for Sustained & United Resistance (ASUR) for hosting epistolary writing workshops in San Francisco and Oakland, CA.

To those who sent letters, as a part of the original *dear Gerald* project, I appreciate you for sharing your fatherlessness with me. We are kin.

Mom, thank you for keeping connections alive for me to later explore. Aubrey, thank you for being a guide and bridge to my paternal line. To my father, Gerald, I am grateful for the "madness" you've given me.

Kate Angus, editor extraordinaire, thank you for understanding how to edit and bring forth my genius. Joe Pan, thank you for believing in this manuscript.

Adrian Blevins, Roger Bonair-Agard, Melissa Febos, Alexis Pauline Gumbs, Terrance Hayes, Patricia Smith, Emerson Whitney, and

Dara Wier, your beauty, writing, and literary citizenship have inspired and fueled me. Thank you for being my first readers and endorsing the work.

Paul Rammer, your somatic psychotherapy help me to navigate, make it through, and reframe those challenging moments of my Saturn return. Thank you.

To my wife, Samantha, I am deeply grateful for your ability to model the courage and patience needed to heal and grow relationships. You've been a good teacher.

## About the Author

**Arisa White** is a Cave Canem fellow and the author of the full-length poetry collections *You're the Most Beautiful Thing That Happened*, *A Penny Saved*, and *Hurrah's Nest*. Her poetry has been nominated for a Lambda Literary Award, NAACP Image Award, California Book Award, and Wheatley Book Award. The chapbook *"Fish Walking" & Other Bedtime Stories for My Wife* won the inaugural Per Diem Poetry Prize. She's the coauthor of *Biddy Mason Speaks Up*, winner of the Maine Literary Book Award for Young People's Literature and the Nautilus Book Award Gold Medal for Middle-Grade Nonfiction. As the creator of the Beautiful Things Project, Arisa curates poetic collaborations that center narratives of queer people of color. She serves on the board of directors for Foglifter and Nomadic Press and is an assistant professor of creative writing at Colby College. Find her at arisawhite.com.